Linda; She is not my wife

Simon Rieber

ISBN 978-93-5667-378-6
© Simon Rieber 2023
Published in India 2023 by Pencil

Contributors:
Co-Author: Simon Rieber

A brand of
One Point Six Technologies Pvt. Ltd.
123, Building J2, Shram Seva Premises,
Wadala Truck Terminal, Wadala (E)
Mumbai 400037, Maharashtra, INDIA
E connect@thepencilapp.com
W www.thepencilapp.com

Author biography

Simon Cosmas Michael, known professionally as Simon Rieber, is an Tanzanian visual artist, animator and author who uses the fields of folk art. He first gained popularity as an artist on Instagram. He is the winner of the Umoja Prize for Contemporary Tanzanian Artist in 2020. He is the author of How To Draw With Mouse (USING ADOBE ILLUSTRATOR) He is a founder and C.E.O of SR Media Services Tanzania a company helping budding artists, entrepreneurs and creators to promote their works online. he was named "Artist of this generation" with Limitless Magazine

CONTENTS

Chapter one

The first time I saw this girl was one Saturday when I was in our street outside a general store selling films distributed by the Smart Ideas Communications company.

I was impressed by how fresh she was, also clean and looking like a daughter who knows life and has an understanding of life and is also civilized, unlike our daughters in the street.

I say different from the girls in the street, because they used to praise them falsely that they are beautiful, but for them, greeting or even talking to their peers was a taboo and you can probably use more insults than what you read on some Facebook pages.

I remember that period, I had passed my sixth form exam and I was given a gift of a very useful phone that gave me the ability to access Facebook and access other networks.

I asked her name and she told me her name is Linda Fred and she is a stranger to the area, her father has been transferred there for work and she is studying form five in a girls school in the southern regions of Tanzania.

We found ourselves friends and we were often together when I accompanied him to the library to study, sometimes to church and there was a time when he really liked movies so I started to like going to watch movies in various movie theaters that he liked.

Until the day comes to go back to school so that now he goes to start the last year, that is the sixth form, we were already lovers and we had done the things we had done more than four times and in fact we were all swallowed up in the dragon of love together with my family forbidding me but I closed my ears.

Chapter two

Even though his school didn't have a phone, we kept in touch because every weekend he called me and we talked to him happily and comforted each other a lot at that time when the process of going to college was going through for me to apply to various colleges abroad and in the country.

One Monday in an unusual situation I got a call from Linda and she told me that she was in bed suffering from fever, I comforted her that she will recover and I continued to communicate with her.

A few days later the communication was lost and I spent more than two weeks without knowing what to do and I had no other way to get information. Two days later, I received a message from the same security number that Love can run tonight.

Out of fear and surprise, I started dialing the number, it was not received and then it was turned off completely... I had to urinate and I had to go to the toilet outside.

While I was outside, I saw a light indicating in the distance that there is a car coming towards our house. A quick mind told me to climb a big tree that was bringing shade to us to see what was going on.

The car stopped there and the first one to get off was Linda with a father who looked full of exercise and I quickly recognized him as Linda's father. they knocked on the door and father and mother opened it and the old man didn't say a word other than saying I have a problem and where is your child???

Father asked him, what's wrong with my old friend? Linda's father said I have a problem with your son, only you will know what the problem is that brought me here. father told mother to go to the room to call me but unfortunately, they said he was not there but he was in here not long ago.

Linda's father slapped Linda and said you idiot, did you tell him that we are coming??? then he turned to his father and mother and told them to tell him I will come back and he has nowhere to hide or run and then he started the car and left.

Mom and dad sat there for several minutes arguing that I might have made her pregnant or what kind of game was going on and did I run away from the yard I knew they would want?? I made sure they went inside, I went down slowly, I crawled to the window, I bumped into the little guy, he gave me my jacket and pants, and they brought me a small bag and I immediately left.

I left not knowing where I was going but I was hoping that I would find a place to sleep and I had 33,000 shillings/- in my pocket, I entered a hotel and slept then at twelve o'clock I ran and went to the stand and bought a ticket to Chombe without knowing where I was going.

Chapter Three

At that time, all the phones are switched off and I have my mother's bank card which she opened so that we can keep the funds for our egg chicken project at home and there was more than one million in the account so I said I am running in the street.

That evening when I was drunk I had already called a relative whose younger brother I studied with and he received me and welcomed me and then kept me at home and he continued with his work and I used that opportunity to call one of my friends who when I called him I was surprised to hear him crying and he started blaming me now see what you have done to us you have given him Linda's father got pregnant today and here I am at his house, he said I won't leave until you come.

At the same time more than 40 sms came in from father, mother and some other brothers saying don't come back and what have you done now? I called my mother and asked her how things were because she loved me so much, she said that Linda was expelled from school because she is pregnant and her father is a soldier with a very high rank and she said that she will look for me and she also doesn't want anyone but me.

He also added that the father has even tried to take some old people to go and put things right but they have failed and the father hates me and is looking for me. I told mother now I will look for you only myself. I turned off all the phones and broke the lines and bought a new phone line and then it was time to sleep and I fell asleep.

In the morning, I continued to help my brother there and I managed to stay there for a whole week without calling anyone, entering Facebook or giving anyone my number, but to my surprise, the guard's father called me on my phone... telling me not to think that I am hiding, I should come back or in time he will catch me. I shivered with the bitter cold and felt warm.

I came to realize that I was not wearing a shirt when I was approaching Mbeya after Konda demanded that she check the receipt and I groped myself knowing that it was on the shirt but it was not a shirt... I arrived in Mbeya and slept in a hotel and then I called my mother after not contacting her for a week, she told me that it is better to stay here because my father is there and he is tired and wants to look for me now so that I don't kill him for nothing and I used that opportunity to tell him that I have his bank card and he told me to calm down first.

I have been in love for more than a month and I have never been in touch with Linda and even the desire to see her has stopped and no one in the family except my mother knew and now she had to involve my father because my father was called by Linda's father that even if they put me in love, I still haven't run away from more problems I will lose money for the game of hiding while I am seen and he knows all my movements.

My father and mother secretly called me and said that in that situation I can no longer be safe, they sent me a fare and told me to go and meet in Arusha because even my father was now fed up because he tried to resolve without success and the old man only wanted me.

I arrived at Usha at night and slept there. In the morning, I turned on the phone and received an SMS from Linda's father, saying that he is about to throw, don't think that you are hiding too much here.

I started having diarrhea and when mom and dad came in, I was young and I said here now I can die at any time or does the old man have his spies???

Chapter Four

Father and mother stayed with me and we went to a village near Loriondo, there is an old man who said that he has a medicine of spoons, that is, only two spoons, I will not see my father again and he will not know where I am.

I took the medicine as usual and the next day we started the journey back to the house so that I could continue with the process of joining the college because now the dose of spoons would not allow Linda's father to see me again.

I slept a lot when we were approaching the river, I received a message from Linda's father saying that it is very close, I see you are now in the river......... I told my father to stop the car because we had a private transport, I showed them all the sms and they were stunned and I said that I am not going to the house in this style, they will kill me completely with the healer and his spoons are fake

After a long argument, they agreed to stay with my aunt and I stayed there, but on the second day, having courage that I have never had before, I left and went to the house and when I arrived around four o'clock that Saturday, I asked my father and mother and my older and younger father to go to Linda's father house.

We were welcomed to the house and taken to a room where we stayed at that time. I prayed more than seven times and mentioned the names of God for more than ten times while saying that if I am shot or put in a cave then I will never escape.

Linda's father came after about three minutes with a happy face unlike what I thought. He called Linda and put her in there and asked one question "Is this Linda who is pregnant with you?" Linda answered yes.

Then she said, "My parents, please forgive me for what I did. I wanted to find this young man so that I could find out with my ears and you should also listen to what they have planned after the pregnancy?... the parents were stunned and the little father saw that he now blames himself for why he took the knife and hid it as there would be a quarrel.

Linda and I said together that we love each other and we had even planned to study at the same college... and start our lives... the old man said now that I don't want a dowry, I hear you are counting on joining college? If yes, you and your family will help us to take care of him here and also after three months he will have to start a plan to repeat his studies so that he can start college early.

We did that and I managed to start college when I was in the third year. Linda was in the first year and now it's been more than three years since we got married to Linda and the other day, I had the chance to stay with my father-in-law (Linda's father) and I asked him if he was getting information about every place I arrived?

The answer made me feel like a fool... Linda and I installed a software on our phones that if we changed the numbers of the day or even did anything we would get an SMS of the place where the person is and with the help of the network it would show the location and my number set on the phone. so, the old man, since he confiscated the security phone, he got my information every time I changed the line.

HAND OF THE SPY 01

DAR ES SALAAM – Six months ago...

"COMMANDER Amata," a voice called from behind him. He turned and saw Madam S with a file in her hand. He was standing in front of a large house in Gezaulole, his arm covered in a large bandage. He turned and looked at Madam S.

"Yes Mom," he responded and removed his glasses from his face.

"Mr. President congratulates you for the work you have done, he very much accepts your presence here in the country and especially in a sensitive department like this, I have just spoken to him, we have agreed on one thing," he handed him the file on which was written Rhobinson Quebec and underneath it was written 'Wanted' ', he looked at Madam S.
"Only his spirit and we don't call him alive," then he turned and left.

SAD STORY

"It was a long time ago, in 1979, but it was an event that hurt me a lot. It was very difficult to forget it and it made me ask myself, how can God be so cruel. But of course, it was a time of little understanding. Now I know a lot and especially after learn this cognitive knowledge.

It was in 1979 when I was traveling from Dar es Salaam to Arusha. I don't know how it happened, but it happened. We left Dar es Salaam at 12.30 pm. At that time, buses used to travel in the evening and at night, not like these days.

I was going to Arusha for an interview for employment, having just finished the fourth form. I was directly employed by the government, because in those days' jobs were plentiful. However, I was not satisfied with the work I was doing, so I applied for a job at a company in Arusha and was called for an interview.

We arrived at a town called Korogwe which at that time was the most famous town for its hotels along the Segera road to Moshi and Arusha. When we arrived in Korogwe, our bus stopped for passengers to get food. I entered a hotel that I remember to this day that was called Bamboo. I ordered food and ate quickly due to the short eating time given by the owners of the TTBS bus that I traveled with. When I was paying, I was surprised and scared. I put my hand in my pockets and found that I had no change. I started to complain and the owner of the hotel said that he could not accept that ignorance, "Some passengers are crooks, sir, they eat and pretend to be stolen, if you agree with them every day you will only lose" The hotel owner said with determination.

There was a huge commotion, with the hotel owner saying that he must send me to the police. It is true that he sent one of his servants to the police station so that I could be dealt with.

At the hotel there was a man who was sitting on the side with his wife and their children eating. When the gentleman saw that, he sent a servant to call me. I left the counter where I was flirting and came to the gentleman.

He was a young adult, about 50 years old. I greeted him and he responded, I greeted his wife as well. The gentleman asked me the story of the violence and I told him. He asked me now in Arusha how I would live during the interview when I have been robbed of all the money and how would I return to Dar. I told him I was planning how to return to Dar, if the police were there I would be trusted.

As a joke, the gentleman told me that he would give me money to spend in Arusha and when I return to Dar, I should return his money to him.

I remember he gave me 90 shillings with a promise that when I return to Dar, I will take his money to his office. He directed me to his office, Nkuruma street and told me that he has decided to help me because every human being needs the help of another and this life is a cycle. I thanked him and left to run to the bus. The bus was just waiting for me. I boarded the bus and other passengers apologized to me. We left Korogwe, but it didn't take long for our bus to have a problem with one of the front wheels. We had to park in the corner for it to be repaired. After repairs, we left to continue our journey.

Near the town of Same at seven o'clock at night, our bus stopped suddenly. Passengers stood in the bus and there was a kind of pushing. There was an accident outside. The passengers got off quickly and some down there started screaming, especially the women. When I got down, I saw a small black car that was badly crushed and there were two dead bodies on the side.

I knew they were corpses because they were covered in wrinkles. Then there was a baby who was crying a lot with a bandage on his head. Let's take this child to the same hospital, he is hurt, although not too much. I looked at a boy about three years old. he was injured on the forehead, but it was alive. Of course, those were his parents, he was already an orphan. Tears came out of my eyes.

After getting help from the road safety police to take the dead bodies, we boarded the bus to continue our journey. Once upon a time, a child was taken by some relatives who had a government Land Rover to be rushed to the hospital. Inside the bus, the conversation was only about the accident, until we arrived in Arusha. We arrived very late in Arusha because we arrived at five o'clock in the morning, instead of two o'clock.

I slept in a simple hotel and had an interview the next day. It was that day, after the interview, when I bought the newspaper that I had a great shock.

However, the two people who died in the Same accident were the gentleman who helped me and his wife. Their son was the one who survived. I found that out after reading his name and the name of the company when he told me to send him his money on my way back to Dar, along with his picture, wife and child. I cried a lot, like a baby.

I couldn't figure out why he died. I wondered who would raise the child now? They were questions without answers and probably stupid questions too.

I knew that I had a debt, a debt of ninety shillings. At that time, ninety shillings were equal to one hundred thousand shillings today. For the first time now, I wondered why the deceased believed in me and decided to give me the money. I didn't get an answer.

I cut the piece of the English newspaper that contained the news. I took the piece and put it in my Diary. Debt, how would I pay people's debt? I found myself kneeling and asking God to give me the ability to come and pay the good man's debt in any way. 'God, please come and enable me to pay the debt of the deceased in the way and manner you know.

I want to pay this debt so that I have done something for the deceased,' I prayed. I returned to Dar the same day. Because of many things and especially after the results of the interview were bad for me, I found myself with many things and quickly forgot about the person who helped me who is late. However, I managed to get a chance to study at the Cement College and then the technical college and finally I was lucky enough to go to England. In 1991 I started my activities.

It was in 1995 when I was in my office where was the Nasaco building that burned down in 1996, where it was rebuilt and renamed Water Front. While I was doing my work, I was told by my secretary that there was a young man who wanted to see me.

I asked him which boy, he said he didn't know. I told him to let him in. The young man entered the office. He was a young man about 17 or 18 years old, white and a little tall. He was wearing the best he could, that is, casually while his health was not very satisfactory.

I welcomed him for as long as possible, because I saw that he would waste my time. I have to be honest that I was not a very compassionate person and I believed a lot in people with money or names. I asked him, "what can I help you with, young man, and if you do it quickly, I will be grateful because I have a meeting in a short time". I said I didn't have any session, but I just wanted him to leave quickly.

"I'm sorry, old man, I had a problem...I've been kicked out of school and I don't have anyone to help me anymore because...I'm...I'm in the second form and that's all I'm looking for if someone shows up.... I cut him off. "Listen boy.

If you have nothing else to say, you'd better let me do the work. Do you think that if I decide to help everyone who was expelled from school, I will not return to our place on foot! Go to the Ministry of Education and tell them. First, what are your parents doing, why should they fail... Why did they send you to a paid school if they don't have the ability, they want reputation?"

"No, my parents died and I study in a government school. I lack the basic needs and school fees. I study in Kwiro, Morogoro. My aunt is the one who teaches me, and she has cancer and now she doesn't even work.," She started crying.

Some compassion came over me and I said to myself, if it's just fare and use, why not be kind, at least for once. "When did father and mother die?" I asked knowing that they would have died of AIDS, because that period was when the fashion of AIDS started, where everyone who dies is considered to have died of AIDS.

"They died in an accident when I was very young, when I was three years old. Yes, my aunt took me and raised me until now she is dying of cancer." The boy cried more. I would like to tell you, the reader who is reading here, that there is a certain power and now I believe that there are many that lead our lives without us knowing.

Something hit my mind! I found myself asking Yuel the boy. "Why did you decide to come to me, who directed you here and what year and where did your parents die?" The young man said, "I thought I should just try for anyone who can help me, and that's how I found myself entering here, I don't know.... I wasn't sent by anyone. My parents died in 1979 in Same and they say I was in an accident, I survived. I was only hurt here." He touched the scar on his forehead.

I felt something rise in my stomach and come to my chest and then I felt as if I was suffocated and unable to breathe. "What was your father's name?" "His name was Siame.Cosmas Siame." I stood up suddenly until the young man was shocked. I went to my cupboard in the office and rummaged through one of the drawers and came out with a diary. Hands shaking, I took out a piece of newspaper in the diary, which I had kept.

"Yes, his name was Cosmas Siame. This is his son, the one who survived." I whispered. I found myself kneeling and praying. "God, you are powerful and nothing can defeat you. I have believed father that every good thing we do is our savings for tomorrow and that tomorrow starts here on earth." Then I fell silent and cried a lot. I cried with joy and the discovery of the power that touches a human being in everything he does.

I stood up perfectly balanced. I felt like a completely different person. I followed the boy and hugged him while I was still crying. "I am your little father; I will raise you now. It is my turn now to raise you until the end" And he cried without knowing the reason and was completely confused. I went back to the chair and told him what happened 17 years ago.

We left there and went to see his aunt Ubungo, the dairy area where she had booked a room. Due to his condition, I transferred him to me, after telling him what happened. Cosmas' sister was so happy that she couldn't speak for an hour. He died however a year later, but very satisfied.

Siamese young man studied and finished University and is currently in Australia where he works. The truth is that he is completely my son now. I believe that in Heaven his parents are enjoying what they planted many years ago. But I still wonder. How did Cosmas give me that help? Then I wonder what drew Siame's son to my office bypassing all other offices? I want to tell you, don't be too cynical for no reason, there are additional forces that lead to results in our lives.... THOSE POWERS ARE THE LOVE OF GOD! "

T.S.A HEADQUARTERS 1999

"Do you drink tea or coffee?" Gina asked a question to Amata who was stunned, staring at the computer scrolling through this and that.

"Your same question every day, and my answer always the same," he answered and they all laughed out loud.

"What are you guys doing there?" Madam S asked as she stood at the door.

They all stood up to give him their respect, "Welcome Madam, you have entered like a shadow!" The commander joked.

"Even a shadow appears, say like air!" he answered and then they all laughed again, "Commander Amata, come to the office after your business, I have something to explain to you and work on it," he left. Amata looked at Gina and then they continued with their laughter and chain a coffee arguments.

"Madam is calling you to the office, is there work?" Gina became aggressive.

"No, there would be a job he would send you and all of you would be in a frenzy of planning that job, he would want to ask me if I would marry you or not," Amata replied.

"Mmmmmm! That marriage between me and you will be a hook," Gina continued the conversation and gave Amata a cup of coffee.

In front of the computer, Amata was sitting without talking to anyone, no one knew what he was looking for except him alone. When he came to finish his work and looked up, he found himself alone with a cold coffee on the table. He raised his walkie talk and called.

"Hey, come here, we are in room number five," Gina called Amata even before she was told anything.

In the room there were four people, Madam S, Gina, Jasmine and Amata, sat watching one of the heavy spy movies that you can't look at twice with your light soul. For them, the game taught them a lot, especially in internal and external sports.

It was showing thirty-nine Intelligence steps, each one was sitting quietly following the movie which had a lot of training. When it ended after ninety minutes, everyone took a deep breath and looked at Madam S who was sitting quietly with her hand resting on her chin. He got up and looked at them all.

"I am about to disgrace your mother, age has given me a hand, be ready for anything from now on." Commander, come to the office,"

Amata got up and followed Madam S to her office, a wide office with enough space, it had six clean chairs, a large wooden table carved by Suma J.K.T's youth made the office beautiful. On the wall hung a large picture of the late Father of the Nation, and in the far corner there was a picture of a man with bright eyes who seemed to know a lot of things. If you look at that picture you can ask a question but it was a picture. Although Commander Amata was T.S.A 1, he still entered this office very few times. The picture that was there reminded him of Mogadishu when he met the man The Chameleon, he wanted to tell Madam S about it but still his covenant with the fake deceased was to keep a secret.

Madam S went around the back of the table, stood in front of the big national flag that was on her right and on her left, there was a big T.S.A logo, a logo that carried the national shield and was engraved with pure gold on its edge, on it appeared the head of a Giraffe which was preceded and the glacier of Mount Kilimanjaro. At the bottom of the emblem, the three letters T.S.A were carried over two spears that made an X symbol.
"At four o'clock this evening, there is a sensitive meeting at the Ministry of Foreign Affairs and International Cooperation, I will go there, but I want to see you as soon as I leave, if there is anything different, I will shock you, be ready all the time," Madam told him while standing upright.

"Yes! Madam, I am always ready,"

"There is a big, very difficult job ahead of you, Amata, which will put your life in a mortgage more than ever, but you have to do it, and we will be shoulder to shoulder with you,"

"Yes, Madam," he answered firmly.

"Now I am going to see the Honorable Minister and then I will call you to the office so that we can see what we are doing in this, because even I still do not know but I have only hinted about it," Madam finished her explanation.

In the evening of that day, Commander Amata D.D.C Kariakoo found himself getting one or two colds, his mind wandered as well, he found himself gripped by a big lump to know what is going to happen in their office. He was used to being told all the work directly by Madam S and started it at the same time, but he was surprised now that Madam S gave him a note and told him I will call you later.

The beer went down slowly but it didn't cause any trouble in the young man's brain, it went down like water and made him want to go to the bathroom several times. The Tanzanian music that was being played by Msondo's band made him lose his thoughts for a moment and not a second. He entertained himself by singing a little but when his thoughts returned to what he was eagerly waiting for. He looked at his watch, it was already half past eleven in the evening, the sun had left the city and when you looked at it, it was setting in the Pugu mountains. He got up and went through the middle of the crowd, went straight out of the exit gate, went down the stairs and went to his car which he parked right next to the Indian shop.

Just as he was sitting on the chair, his phone rang, he picked it up and looked at it, Chiba, fired it and put it to his ear.

"What's up boy, is the holiday over?"

"Oh, our offices don't have holidays, if a deal happens anywhere and at any time, you add yourself," Chiba replied.

"Tell me!"

"How's the weather there?" Chiba asked.

"Pako shwari, I'm hiding in the hut, just spray," the Commander told him.

"Brother, what is there? Because Madam, I'm telling you to go back, here I am, I'm already at Mauritius Airport, I'm going back," Chiba explained.

"Aaaah! I can see that this lady is getting old now, I myself told her to wait and she will call me," the Commander informed her.

"Ok, in the next four hours I will be at Dar, brother,"

"And the Mauritian motto?" The commander joked.

"No, just myself, I leave that here, over!" Chiba finished speaking, by saying the word over he meant that the conversation should not continue.

"See you Ruvuma to Maputo in the next 500 minutes, over!" The commander hung up the phone and returned to his place, then slowly entered the road and left the area.

He always did not like to stay in one place for a long time. He entered Msimbazi road and headed towards Faya, where he turned right to follow Morogoro road until near the Technical College of Dar es Salaam, turned left and took Ally Khan dirt road, passed Zanaki and continued to Red Carpet restaurant, parked his car outside and going down, he looked around and then closed the door while leaving the car keys inside.

MINISTRY OF FOREIGN AFFAIRS AND INTERNATIONAL COOPERATION

"Madam S," Mr. Francis Kifaru called with his heavy voice burdened by his previous obesity. He was always sitting as if he was drowsy due to his advanced age. "Old people like these are just disgraced, they cling to power until they die in office, that's why the country is not progressing" Madam thought.

"Yes, Sir," he said.

"As I told you, that and those relatives have asked us to help them and if it's not as we ask them, then it's our turn, I believe your department will do well," the Old Man gave instructions and gave Madam S a folder with several papers in it with the text Top Secret, she quickly looked at it and to put it well.

"Ok, the work has reached its place and will be carried out," he answered and said goodbye to the old man, then went out.
When she sat in the car, she calmed down first, "very clean, now there is only one job, I was thinking a lot about this barbarian" Madam S thought to herself as she pulled

her car out of the parking lot.

Musanda, Pretoria - a. south

DUMISAN SAJAK MBEKHI, the chief leader of the South African Intelligence Service (NIA) remained as still as frozen in his big desk in the office. Darkness had already ruled the city of Pretoria, a peaceful and quiet city in South Africa.

While he was still in deep thought, the door of his office was pushed open, and a young woman with a medium body, neither tall nor short, entered wearing a military uniform. When he stood in front of his host, while they were separated from the big table, he left his hat on his shoulders and put it on his head. then he stood stiffly.

Dumisan stood up looking clearly furious with anger and revenge.

"Debra, I don't need to waste time, I have appointed you because I know your profile in the army, you should leave tonight on a British plane, go to Canada, there is someone you need to kill and then come back immediately. I want you to kill him and nothing else, I expect good answers from you, thank you." Dumisan sat down. Debra saluted and left the office, she didn't have to answer anything because that was an order, all she had to do was carry out what she was told then.

TO BE CONTINUE...................